D1597062

"I am no bird; and no net ensnares me:
I am a free human being with an independent will."

– Charlotte Brontë, *Jane Eyre*

KinderGuides™ Early Learning Guides to Culture Classics
Published by Moppet Books
Los Angeles, California

ISBN: 978-0-9988205-0-7

Art direction and book design by Melissa Medina
Written by Melissa Medina and Fredrik Colting

Printed in China

www.moppetbookspublishing.com

Kinder Guides

EARLY LEARNING GUIDE TO **CHARLOTTE BRONTË'S**

JANE EYRE

By MELISSA MEDINA *and* FREDRIK COLTING

Illustrations by MADALINA ANDRONIC

MOPPET BOOKS

Table *of* Contents

About *the* Author

CHARLOTTE BRONTË was born in 1816 in Northern England, into a very talented family. In fact, she and her younger sisters, Emily and Anne, all became famous writers. The three sisters and their brother, Branwell, would entertain each other as children by writing fantastic stories about imaginary kingdoms. Charlotte also especially liked to write poems, but she is most well known for writing the novel *Jane Eyre* in 1847. Though for this story she didn't make up a magical kingdom. Instead, she wrote a story that was based on many of her own experiences. At first she published it under the name Currer Bell because back then women writers were not taken as seriously as men. How silly! We have Charlotte and her sisters to thank for paving the way for today's female writers.

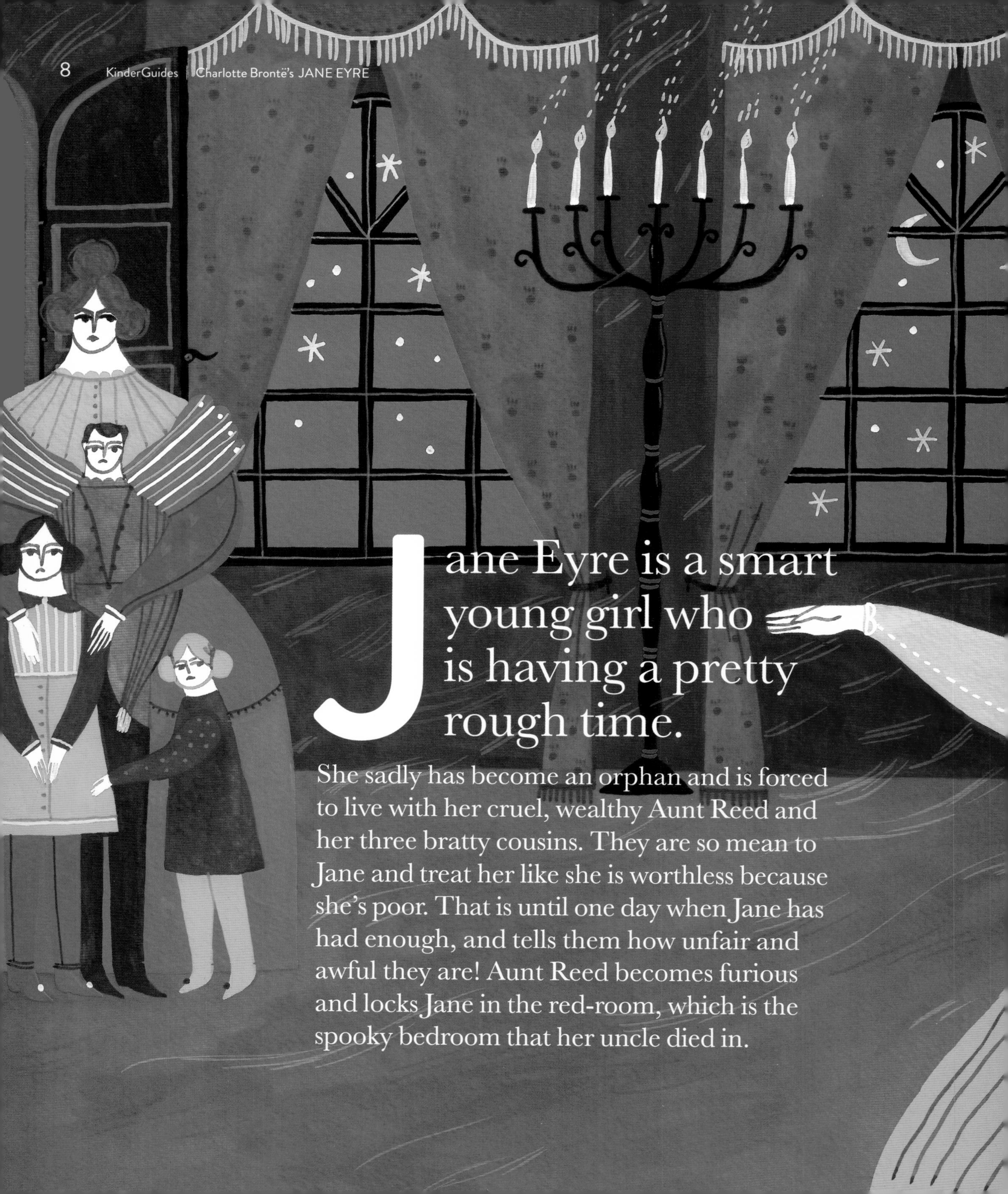

Jane Eyre is a smart young girl who is having a pretty rough time.

She sadly has become an orphan and is forced to live with her cruel, wealthy Aunt Reed and her three bratty cousins. They are so mean to Jane and treat her like she is worthless because she's poor. That is until one day when Jane has had enough, and tells them how unfair and awful they are! Aunt Reed becomes furious and locks Jane in the red-room, which is the spooky bedroom that her uncle died in.

Jane thinks she sees her uncle's ghost and gets so scared that she passes out!

After this, Aunt Reed decides Jane is too much trouble and sends her away to a boarding school.

At first, life at the Lowood boarding school is not much better because it's run by a greedy headmaster named Mr. Brocklehurst, who does not give the children enough food or warm clothes. Luckily, Jane becomes friends with a nice girl named Helen who makes things more bearable.

Helen is a very kind, spiritual person and she encourages Jane to stay strong and not lose faith. For instance, one day mean Mr. Brocklehurst gets mad at Jane and makes her stand on a stool all day, forbidding the other girls to talk to her. Jane is humiliated, but Helen assures her that the other students are on her side and that she's not alone.

Jane is so happy to have a best friend, and just as she is learning to make the best of things, something awful happens: a bunch of the girls at school get sick, including Helen, who eventually dies in Jane's arms. Jane is so sad to lose her sweet friend. The school board blames Mr. Brocklehurst for not keeping the children well, and he is fired! Good riddance!

Luckily, some nice people take over his position and things finally start to improve at Lowood. Jane does really well at her studies, and becomes especially good at drawing. She stays at Lowood for six more years and even becomes a teacher

Jane is now a young woman and is ready for a change. She takes a job at a big estate called Thornfield Hall to work as a governess for a young French girl named Adèle. Her adoptive father is a mysterious man named Edward Rochester who is usually away in Europe. The nice housekeeper, Mrs. Fairfax, introduces Jane to Adèle and shows her around. Jane finds Adéle to be a sweet girl that likes to learn and Thornfield to be a pleasant place.

There is something strange about it though. At night Jane hears a creepy laughter coming from the third floor. The housekeeper tells her that's just a kooky seamstress named Grace who works in the house.

One restless evening, Jane decides to go for a walk to look at the moon. Suddenly she hears a horse come galloping toward her. Then she sees that the horse has a rider. As they get closer the horse slips on a patch of ice, and the rider falls off!

Jane quickly helps the rider up. He's a stern looking man with rude manners, but still, she thinks there is something intriguing about him. He rides off, but when Jane gets back to the house she sees the mysterious man inside. It's Mr. Rochester!

Now that Rochester is back home, life is more interesting for Jane. He likes her drawings and likes talking to her in front of the fire each night. Jane is a bit surprised that a wealthy, worldly man like Rochester would enjoy talking to a simple governess like her. But she is not scared of him like the other servants, and enjoys his company too. Although there is still something strange about him, like he is hiding a secret.

One night Jane hears the creepy laughter again and she goes to check it out. In the hallway she sees smoke billowing out of Rochester's bedroom, so she runs in to find him asleep with his bed on fire! Jane immediately puts out the flames, and Rochester thanks her for saving his life. He says that it was probably that sneaky Grace who started the fire. But why would she do that?

The next day, no one mentions the fire, which Jane finds odd. Instead, she soon hears that Rochester has invited his wealthy friends to stay at Thornfield for several days. One of the guests is a beautiful woman named Blanche Ingram, who is snobby and mean to Jane. She wants to marry Rochester for his money, and wants to make Jane jealous.

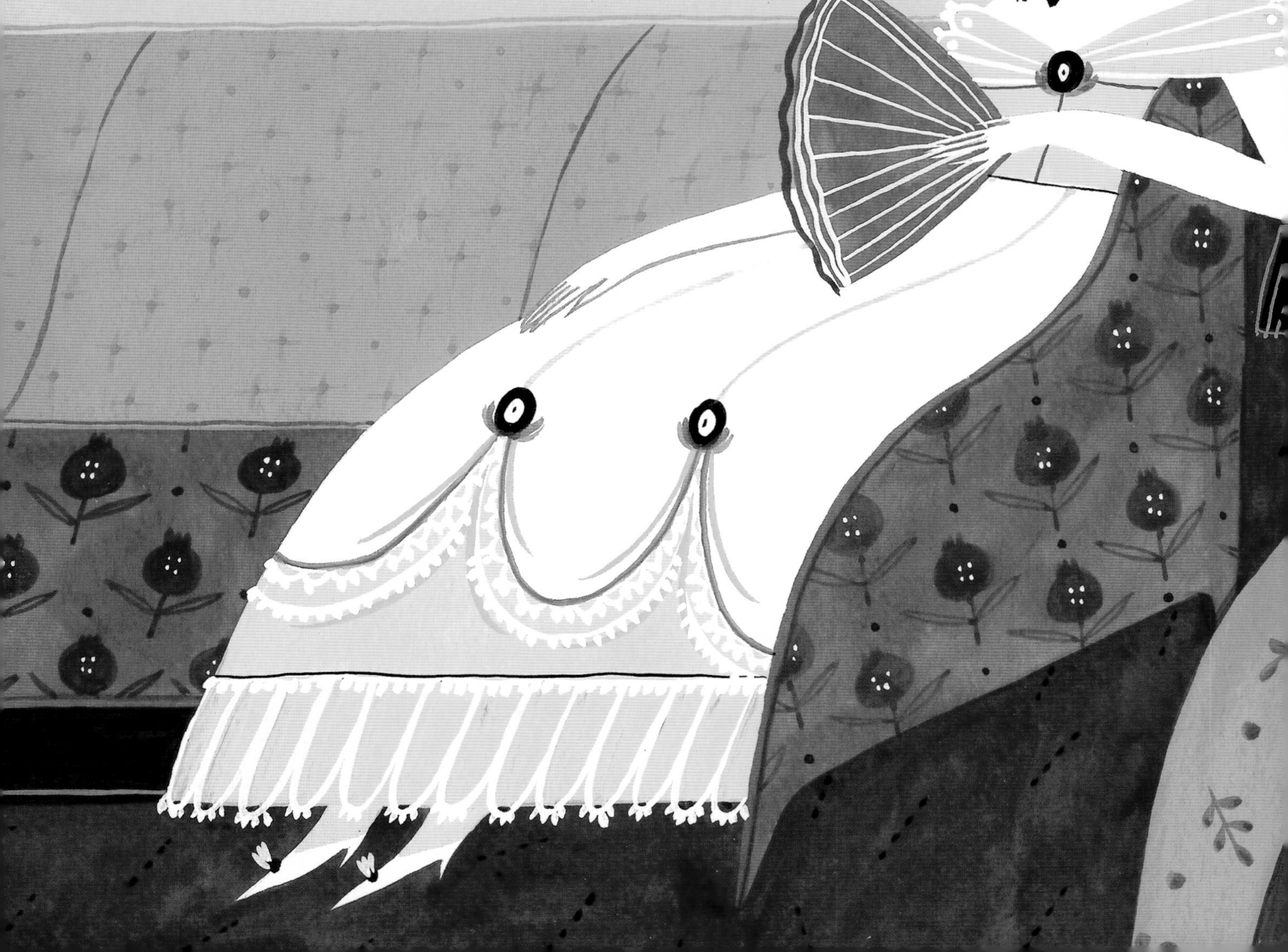

One night, a gypsy woman comes to read their fortunes. She tells Blanche that Rochester is not as rich as she thinks he is, which makes Blanche cranky. Then it's Jane's turn, and the woman tells her that happiness is just around the corner for her. As she keeps talking, her voice gets deeper and Jane realizes that the gypsy is actually Rochester playing a trick on everyone!

Around this time a man named Richard Mason shows up, and Jane notices that Rochester almost seems afraid of him.

That night, after everyone has gone to bed, Jane hears someone cry out. Then Rochester knocks on her door and asks her to come help him. It seems Mason has been up to the third floor and he's been bitten and stabbed in the arm! Was it sneaky Grace again? Jane doesn't have time to find out because she has to help Rochester tend to Mason's wounds until the doctor comes to take him away.

After Mason leaves, Rochester talks to Jane and it seems like he might explain everything, but he just ends up confusing her even more.

The next morning, Jane hears that her Aunt Reed is deathly ill. Even though Aunt Reed treated Jane horribly when she was a little girl, Jane is a kind person, so she goes to visit. While there, Aunt Reed shows Jane a letter that her uncle John sent three years ago saying that he wanted to adopt Jane and someday leave his fortune to her. Aunt Reed had cruelly kept it a secret until now.

As she goes back to Thornfield, Jane realizes something amazing–she is in love with Rochester! But she doesn't think that he could ever love someone as poor and plain as she is. When she arrives she sees that Rochester has bought a big fancy carriage, which everyone thinks he will give to Blanche as a wedding present. But everyone is wrong. It's Jane whom he loves and proposes to, not Blanche!

The day of the wedding arrives, and although Jane is happy, she also feels a bit uneasy for some reason. She can sense that something strange is about to happen.

Well, she's right! Suddenly, in the middle of the ceremony, Richard Mason shows up with a lawyer. They tell Jane that she can't marry Rochester because he is already married! Rochester is furious, but admits that it's true. He is married to another woman, but he says that he has a good explanation.

Rochester takes everyone back to Thornfield and up to the third floor. He opens a secret door and reveals a wild looking woman who is being restrained. He explains that this is Bertha Mason, Richard Mason's sister, whom he married fifteen years ago. She was a nice, beautiful woman back then, and their parents persuaded them to marry to seal the family fortunes. But she soon became mentally ill and violent, so Rochester decided to keep her in the secret upstairs room with her nurse, Grace, so she would be safe.

Now Jane understands that it wasn't Grace she heard laughing at night, it was Bertha! And it was Bertha who set fire to Rochester's bedroom and who bit and stabbed her own brother!

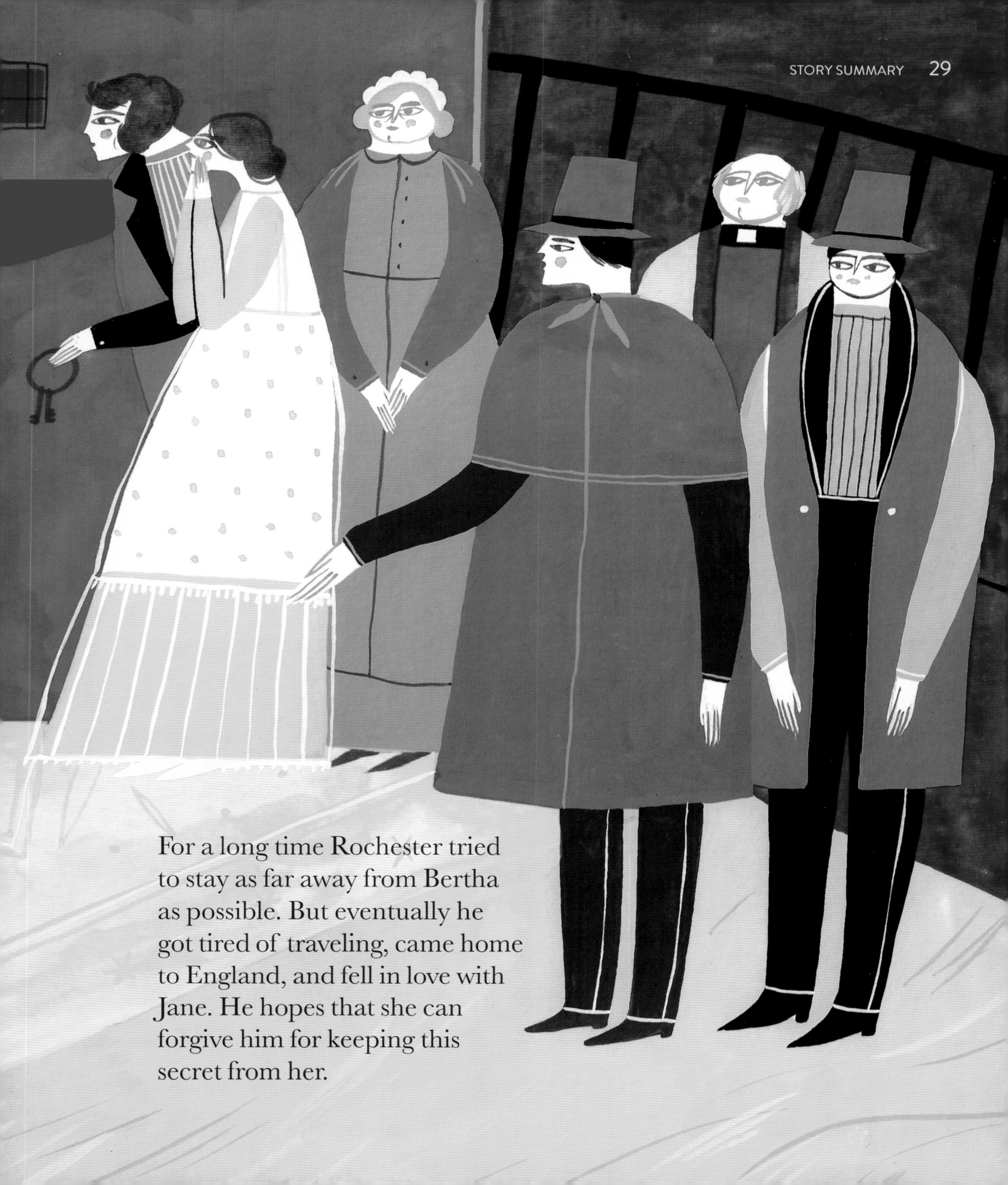

For a long time Rochester tried to stay as far away from Bertha as possible. But eventually he got tired of traveling, came home to England, and fell in love with Jane. He hopes that she can forgive him for keeping this secret from her.

Jane feels sorry for Rochester, but she is overwhelmed by all this news and decides to leave Thornfield the next morning.

Jane has no family and little money, so she doesn't quite know where to turn. She wanders through the moors for days without having anything to eat, until finally, she sees the light of a little house in the distance. She makes it to the front door, then collapses from weakness.

St. John Rivers lives there with his two sisters, Diana and Mary. They open the door and feel so sorry for Jane that they take her in and care for her until she regains her strength.

Jane becomes great friends with the Rivers sisters, and although St. John is not quite as friendly, he does help her get a teaching job at a nearby school.

One day she finds out that the Rivers' father lost all their family money in a bad business deal, and the inheritance they thought they would get from their uncle John has gone to some other relative that they've never met.

Wait a minute–they're talking about Jane! She realizes that the Rivers are her cousins.

It seems she's not alone in the world after all!

Jane generously shares the inheritance with her newfound cousins because they have been so nice to her.

Some time later, St. John tells Jane that he is going to be a missionary in India and that she should go with him. Jane is tempted to say yes because it would be an adventure, but she doesn't like how bossy and cold St. John has become. She tells him no, but he doesn't give up easily.

After dinner, St. John again tries to convince Jane to come to India with him. But all of the sudden, as if in a dream, she hears Rochester calling her name!

Jane has never stopped thinking about Rochester, and now she has to find out if it was really him calling her name. So the next morning she goes back to Thornfield, but she is shocked at what she sees. It has burned to the ground!

She finds Rochester nearby and he explains that after she left, he searched for her everywhere because he didn't want to live without her. Then one night, Bertha set the house on fire again, only this time they couldn't stop it. Although he tried to save her, Bertha died and he became blind from all the smoke. Jane promises that she will never leave him again, and they are so happy to be back together!

They again have a small wedding, only this time there are no interruptions! Jane is happy that she now has her own fortune and family to share with Rochester.

In fact, perhaps it's because Jane cares for him so well, or for other reasons, but Rochester eventually gets his sight back! And once again he can look at his beautiful wife, Jane Eyre.

Main Characters

Jane Eyre

is a smart young woman who longs for both freedom and love. She always tries to do the right thing, and overcomes many hardships to become a teacher and an independent woman.

Edward Rochester

is the mysterious master of Thornfield Hall. Although he can be arrogant and insensitive at times, he is also passionate, wildly in love with Jane and a great guy, once you get to know him.

St. John Rivers

is Jane's rather cold and unfeeling cousin who is a minister and wants Jane to be just like him.

Mary & Diana Rivers

are St. John's sisters. They are kind and intelligent and take care of Jane when she is sick.

Helen

is Jane's friend at Lowood. She is very spiritual and inspires Jane to have faith and stay strong.

Mr. Brocklehurst

is the wicked and greedy Lowood headmaster.

Aunt Reed

is Jane's cruel aunt who sends her away to boarding school when she is a child.

Blanche Ingram

is a beautiful socialite who selfishly wants to marry Rochester for his money.

Mrs. Fairfax

is Thornfield's all-knowing, friendly housekeeper.

Adéle

is Mr. Rochester's adopted daughter for whom Jane is hired to be a governess.

Bertha Mason

is Rochester's violent, insane and secret wife who lives in a hidden room.

Richard Mason

is Bertha's brother who always seems to show up unannounced.

Key Words

GOTHIC FICTION

This is a fancy name for a type of popular English literature from the late 1700s and 1800s that is both spooky and romantic–just like *Jane Eyre*!

ORPHAN

Jane's parents died when she was a child, making her an orphan. In fact, she feels like she doesn't have any family at all for most of the book.

RED-ROOM

The red-colored room where Jane's uncle died that terrified her as a child–especially when she would get locked in there.

GOVERNESS

This is what they used to call a woman hired to teach children in a private household. Jane is Adéle's governess.

THORNFIELD HALL

The big, grand, castle-like home of Mr. Rochester, where most of the story takes place.

THE MOORS

The large grassy fields in Northern England that Jane crosses by foot when she leaves Thornfield.

INHERITANCE

Money or property that is left to someone when their loved one dies. Jane's nice uncle John leaves her a big inheritance.

SUPERNATURAL

That's when something spooky happens that can't be explained by nature or science. Even though most of the spooky stuff in *Jane Eyre* has an explanation, it still seems supernatural at the time!

Quiz Questions

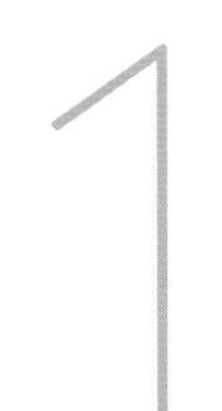

Which room is Jane locked in by her mean aunt?

A. The red-room

B. The blue-room

C. The class room

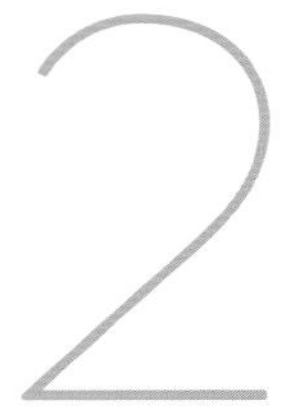

To what school is Jane sent as a little girl?

A. Middlebranch

B. Hightree

C. Lowood

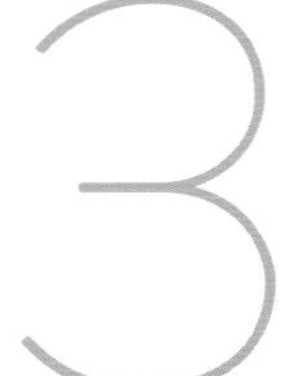

Who is Jane hired to teach?

A. Helen

B. Adéle

C. Charlotte

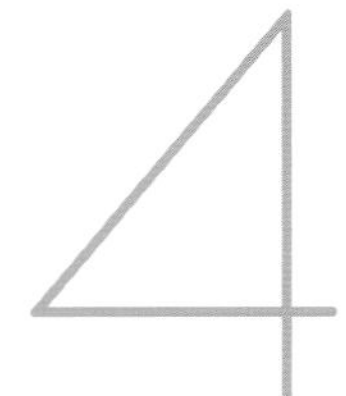

What happens the first time Jane meets Mr. Rochester?

A. He falls from his horse

B. He asks her to dance

C. He sets the house on fire

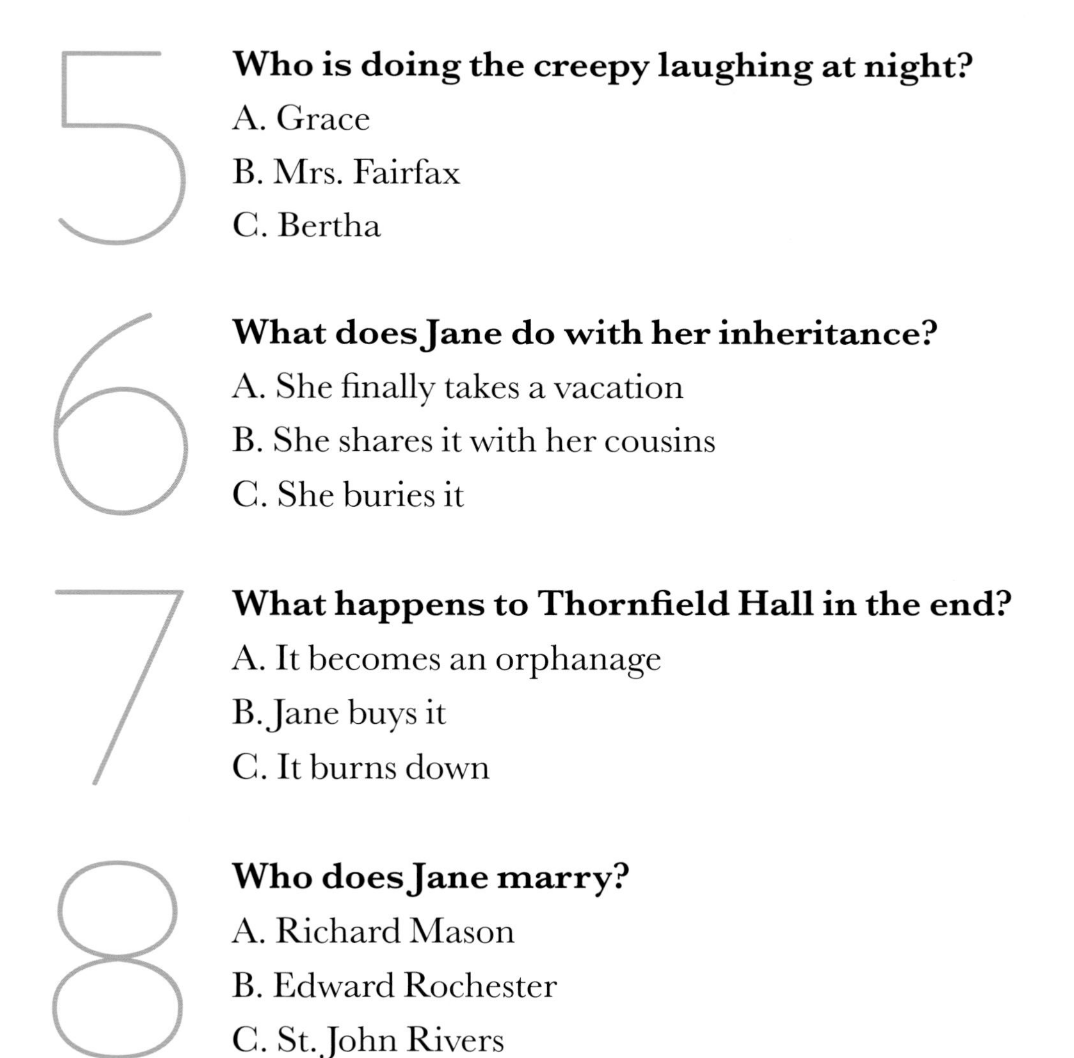

Who is doing the creepy laughing at night?

A. Grace

B. Mrs. Fairfax

C. Bertha

What does Jane do with her inheritance?

A. She finally takes a vacation

B. She shares it with her cousins

C. She buries it

What happens to Thornfield Hall in the end?

A. It becomes an orphanage

B. Jane buys it

C. It burns down

Who does Jane marry?

A. Richard Mason

B. Edward Rochester

C. St. John Rivers

ANSWER KEY:
1:A / 2:C / 3:B / 4:A / 5:C / 6:B / 7:C / 8:B

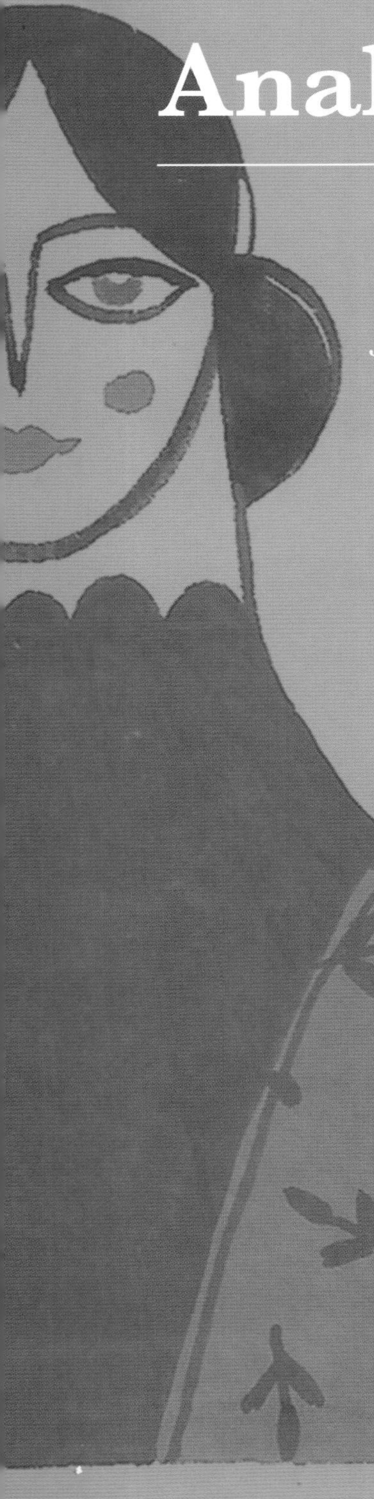

Analysis

Jane Eyre is a book about a girl named…yep, Jane Eyre! It is considered one of the most famous Gothic Fiction books of all time, which means it is spooky and romantic, and has lots of mysterious things that happen in it. We follow Jane from childhood to adulthood as she figures out how to be a good person, even when life seems pretty crummy. From being a poor orphan, abused by her own relatives, banished to an awful school, and finally falling in love just to find out the guy already has a wife–Jane really sees her share of misery! But she never loses her faith. Having faith is believing that things will work out, even when everything seems to be going wrong. Jane's hardships make her strong, independent, and capable of taking care of herself. She is determined to be successful regardless of the difficult situations in her life. Back when *Jane Eyre* was written, there weren't a lot of strong female characters with opinions and dreams, like Jane, so she was ahead of her time!

Jane Eyre is also a love story, although an unexpected one. Rochester is very wealthy and Jane is very poor. He is a world traveler and she has never left Northern England. He is bold and often arrogant while Jane is calm and reserved. But do you know why they fall for each other? Because they connect on a spiritual level, as if they can see right into each other's souls! Rochester likes that Jane is a smart, confident woman who is not afraid to talk to him as an equal, which was not something that most women did back then–especially the hired help! But Jane doesn't care about social status or wealth, she cares about HIM, and she has a good heart. Rochester loves Jane because she is real with him and because she has principles. And in the end, they are finally reunited, this time as equals–just the way Jane hoped it would be.

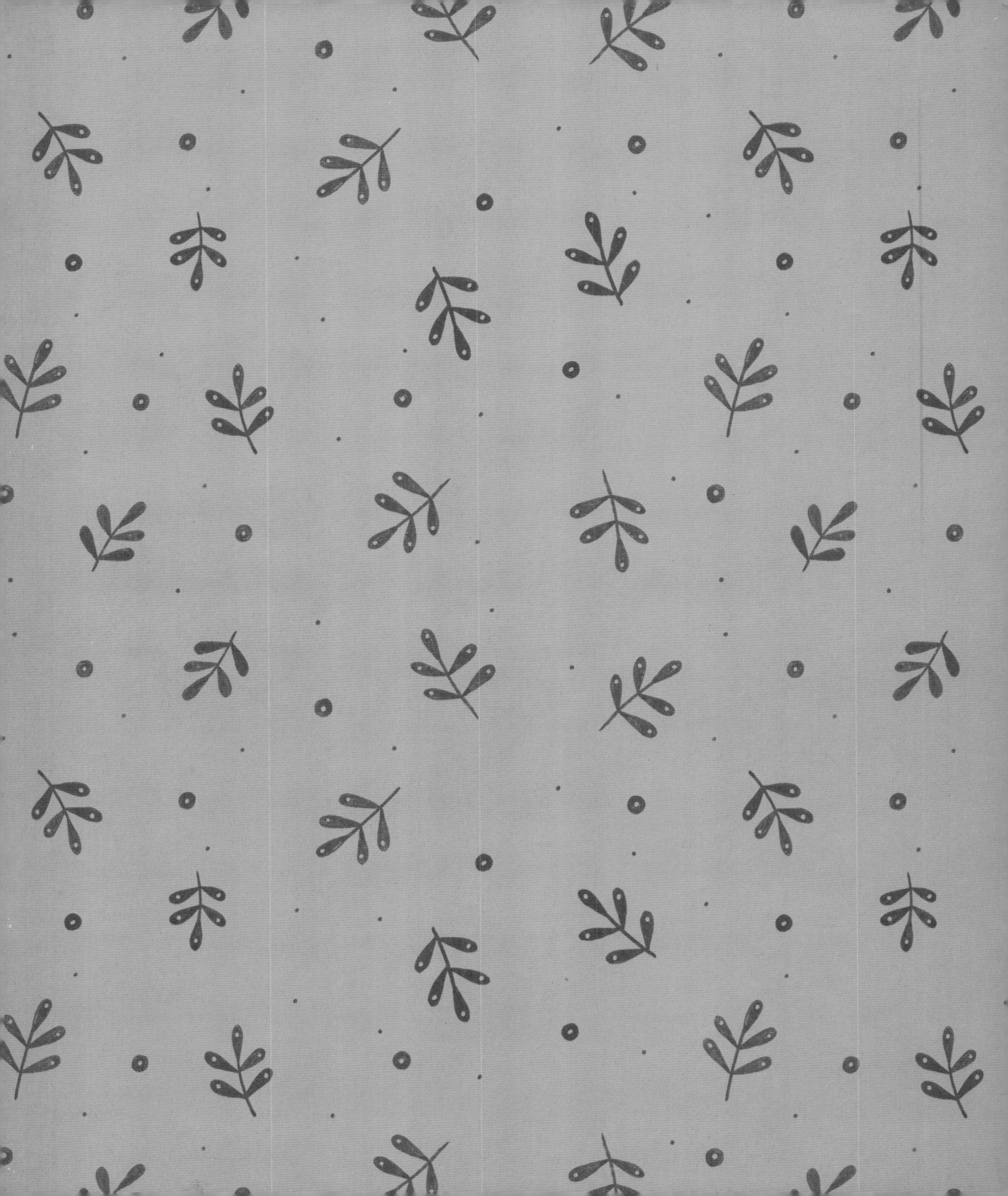